THE OLD COUNTRY

THE OLD COUNTRY

ALAN BENNETT

FABER AND FABER

LONDON   BOSTON

First published in 1978
by Faber and Faber Limited
3 Queen Square London WC1N 3AU
Printed in Great Britain by
Latimer Trend & Company Ltd Plymouth
All rights reserved

All rights whatsoever in this play are strictly
reserved and applications for permission to perform it,
etc. must be made in advance, before rehearsals begin,
to Chatto and Linnit Limited, The Globe Theatre,
Shaftesbury Avenue, London W1

British Library Cataloguing in Publication Data

Bennett, Alan, b. 1934
The old country.
I. Title
822'.9'14   PR6052.E50/

ISBN 0-571-11242-0

To Mary-Kay

The cast consists of three married couples:

HILARY
BRON

ERIC
OLGA

DUFF
VERONICA

The Old Country opened at the Queen's Theatre on
Wednesday, 7th September 1977. The cast was
as follows:

HILARY	Alec Guinness
BRON	Rachel Kempson
ERIC	Bruce Bould
OLGA	Heather Canning
DUFF	John Phillips
VERONICA	Faith Brook

Directed by Clifford Williams
Designed by John Gunter
Lighting by Leonard Tucker

The play was presented by Michael Codron

ACT ONE

A broad verandah above a garden, which is not seen. It is a ramshackle place, a kind of open lean-to put together at various times suggesting one of the 'down at heel riding schools, damp bungalows in wizened orchards' described in the text. The furniture is simple and includes a rocking-chair. There are plenty of books about, standing on and under tables and in piles on the floor. The impression should be that the house is so full of books that they have overflowed on to the verandah. The colour and tone of these books is important. They are a library put together in the 1930s and 1940s and should have the characteristic faded pastel colours of books of that period. Many of them are still in their original dustwrappers. There is a piano offstage.

HILARY and BRON are in their early sixties, their colour and tone rather like that of the books, shabby and faded. HILARY is in a stained linen jacket, old flannels and carpet slippers. BRON is dressed in a vaguely artistic way, distinctive but not elegant.

As the curtain rises HILARY is asleep in the rocking-chair.

The sound of Elgar on the gramophone drifts through from an adjoining room. A very English scene. The music stops.

HILARY, sleeping, suddenly shouts out. It is a terrible cry of guilt and despair. He wakes. Sits. Hears the record has ended and leaving the chair rocking goes out to take it off.

For a moment the stage is empty, the chair rocking, then BRON comes up the stairs from the garden as HILARY comes back.

HILARY: I went to sleep.

BRON: Do you wonder? Elgar!

HILARY: I was at home at Hookham. I was alone in the house when suddenly all the lights came on. I knew it was burglars; I could hear them whispering outside. I got everybody into one room . . .

9

BRON: I thought you said you were alone?

HILARY: I was . . . but there were other people there. Somebody started to open the front door so I got behind it with a hammer. I was just bringing the hammer down on his head when he looked up at me and smiled. It was Pa. Then we were all somehow at a garden party. (*He has been reading a bookseller's catalogue, which he picks up again.*) Anyway I *like* Elgar.

BRON: You don't like Elgar.

HILARY: I do like Elgar.

BRON: I don't see how anyone can like Elgar. I would prefer anything to Elgar.

(HILARY *starts to get up laboriously.*)

Except Vaughan Williams.

(HILARY *sinks back.*)

I looked up that pretty yellow flower. It's a weed apparently.

HILARY: I like it.

BRON: I don't dislike it. It's just getting a bit big for its boots. I think a blitz is in order.

HILARY: Is it native to these parts?

BRON: 'A determined little creeper' the book says.

HILARY: Botanically at least the world hasn't shrunk.

BRON: Has it shrunk?

HILARY: When it comes to airports and architecture one place may look very much like the next but at least vegetation hasn't gone international. Plants still stay more or less put.

BRON: Have to. Don't have a choice. It's a kind of primrose. Smells fractionally of cat. Anyway that's not true. These trees could be anywhere.

(HILARY *goes to one of the piles of books, with his catalogue.*)

HILARY: People are insane. Thirty pounds. I paid . . .eight-and-six.

BRON: When? In nineteen thirty-three? You never buy any books. You're never going to get rid of the ones you've got. Why go through catalogues?

HILARY: They collect anything now. Even fakes. Here's a special section in which every item is an authentic guaranteed forgery. In which context a fake would need to be the

genuine article. Like a woman at a drag ball. By being exactly what she seems she is the impostor. Soon, one imagines, forgeries *of* forgeries. However.
(*Pause.*)

BRON: I'm terrified I'm not going to see any of the jokes.

HILARY: Who says there'll be jokes? You want help?

BRON: With the jokes?

HILARY: With the lunch. I wonder what we've got in store for them in the way of weather. Doesn't look too promising. Dull but I imagine there'll be a spot of sunshine later. No dramatic change: just a light rational breeze with a promise of gradual improvement. A day for Burke, not for Hobbes. Empirical weather.

BRON: That's not what it said on the forecast. The forecast said thunder. Have you nothing to do?

HILARY: No. I thought I might write to *The Times*. I never have.

BRON: What about?

HILARY: Anything. Everybody else does. That seagull. Sir, Am I right or merely sentimental in thinking that in the old days one saw seagulls exclusively by the sea? Here we are, miles from any shore and there is a seagull.

BRON: Aren't you going to wear a tie?

HILARY: Seagulls on the land, starlings by the shore. Perhaps Nature herself is becoming more liberal, embargoes are lifted, borders dissolved and birds as free to roam as we are.
(*Pause.*)

BRON: You want to look nice. Spruce yourself up a bit.

HILARY: No.

BRON: I miss the sea. It's ages since I saw it.

HILARY: Quite candidly I've never seen the point of the sea. Except where it meets the land. The shore has point, the sea none. Of course when you say you miss the sea that's what you mean: you miss the shore.

BRON: I miss the sea. Chop, chop, chop. How do you know what I miss?

HILARY: Lots of people seem to have died. I could write a note for the obituary column.

BRON: Shall I look you out a tie?

HILARY: Sir, Might I be permitted to pen a footnote to your (otherwise admirably comprehensive) obituary of Sir Derek (Jack) Clements.

BRON: Is he dead?

HILARY: Clem blew into my section sometimes in 'forty-two during those early Heath Robinson days when we still lived over the shop at the old Ministry of Supply. We must have seemed a pretty motley crew: a novelist or two, a sprinkling of dons. There was even a fashionable photographer. It was the sort of shambolic, inspirational kind of outfit that fetched the War Office out in a periodic rash. So when Clem came along with his one leg and Ronald Colman moustache it gave the proceedings a welcome air of respectability.

BRON: He's not dead?

HILARY: Soon after the advent of Clem the tempo quickened. Dieppe, St Nazaire, Arnhem . . . none of them successes in the orthodox sense of the word. But then Clem was never orthodox: that wasn't his way. Throughout his life and particularly in these last trying years he was sustained by the loving kindness of his wife, the famous Brenda. 'More than a wife' he used to say. 'A chum.' A few days before his death he was visited by a friend. 'I'm sorry,' he said, 'I've just pissed the bed. Still,' and his face broke into a grin, 'Free country.' Ah Clem, with you, irony was never far away. The world is a colder place without you. However.

BRON: Is he dead?

HILARY: Years ago.

BRON: You keep doing that. Who was it died the other day? Somebody. I can't remember. You should tell me when people die, otherwise I lose my bearings.

(*Pause.*)

He was the one with the ears?

HILARY: That was Sillitoe.

BRON: He's not dead?

HILARY: No. He lives with his sister in Tewkesbury. Or did. He may be dead . . . I don't know. You can sort it out with Veronica. She'll have all the dirt.

'Praise, my soul, the King of heaven

12

To his feet thy tribute bring'

(*He sings this snatch of a hymn and tails off into silence.*)

BRON: Would you rather they weren't coming?

(*Silence.*)

Would you?

HILARY: Where would you say this landscape could be? Other than here.

BRON: Would you?

HILARY: Where?

BRON: Nowhere.

HILARY: Because given the lie of the land I would have said Scotland.

BRON: Scotland.

HILARY:

List characteristics, natural features,
Available cover to safeguard retreat.
A long fir tree plantation, heather handy for hide-outs.
Odd birch trees give bearings and pinpoint the place.
A house by the forest, the best of grid references,
Smoke from a chimney, the first one for miles.

Scotland, darling. Caledonia, stern and wild. A smiling refuge on the edge of the moors: what the Scots call a policy. A patch of order. Peace amid the wildness of nature. Straight out of John Buchan. The moors baking in the sun of a pre-war summer. A line of beaters advance through the heather, as a single plane climbs slowly in the empty sky and a black car waits at the cross-roads. There is a crashing among the trees and a young man stumbles into the garden, incongruously dressed in a crumpled city suit. 'I say, you look about all in.' The young man eyes them warily. Who are they, this couple? They look ordinary enough. A country doctor perhaps. A retired professor and his wife. Dotty he decides, but harmless, and soon he is tackling a goodly meal of ham and eggs and fresh-baked bread, washed down with lashings of strong tea. In the spotless cottage kitchen he tucks in with a will, not knowing that elsewhere in the house a telephone call is being made. Did the young man but turn his head he would see beaters filtering through the wood as

13

the black car creeps slowly up from the cross-roads. It is a trap, this haven: the place where they had meant him to end up all along. Or a reservoir, property of the East Midlands Water Board. That's where they plant forests like this. To cover something up. A blanket round dumps. Camps. An official forest.

(BRON *goes out.*

HILARY *gets up and looks across the garden, singing another snatch of the same hymn*:)

'Ransomed, healed, restored, forgiven,
Who like me his praise should sing?'

(*He waves.*) Hello! Where've you been hiding yourself? You're quite a stranger. Nothing amiss, I hope? I was just wondering whether I dare venture forth. Doesn't look too promising, does it? Best not go too far afield. Still it's what we need: the dahlias are dying on their feet. However. Soldier on. Don't work too hard.

(BRON *comes back with three ties.*

HILARY *takes one, changes his mind and takes another instead, say a Garrick Club tie.*

Pause.)

If one was a drunkard and one's name was Johnny Walker one could form a society called Alcoholics Eponymous. Or if there were two of you called Johnny Walker, Alcoholics Synonymous. However.

BRON: Are you going to be sitting around here all morning?

(*Pause.*)

What happened to your walk?

(HILARY *shrugs.*

Pause.)

Can't keep up with you. Five minutes ago you were bubbling over.

HILARY: Well now I've bubbled over.

BRON: Pity you couldn't save it.

HILARY: Save what?

BRON: The bubbling over. Been bubbling over when they were here and bubbled over after they'd gone. Or be like me. Always at Gas Mark One.

HILARY: And nothing in the oven. (*He stands up and stretches.*)
　　Oven/haven, given/Devon, leaven/lumpen, open/heaven.
　　Where do birds go when they fly across the sky?
BRON: You've got birds on the brain.
HILARY: Not all birds of course. Some just float around the sky
　　not doing anything in particular. But look, that one. (*He
　　hands* BRON *some binoculars.*) That's quite definitely off on an
　　errand. It's got up early, done its stint in the dawn chorus,
　　looked at its wrist watch and set off somewhere. Now where?
　　I think it's late for an appointment with the headmaster of a
　　good comprehensive school that might possibly be persuaded
　　to admit its child on the strength of its slight proficiency on
　　the cello and the prominence of its father in the field of
　　communications. Whereas that one, flying round and round
　　in seemingly aimless circles, is in some agitation over the
　　proposed demolition of several quite pleasant, though not
　　architecturally outstanding Victorian villas in order to make
　　room for some old people's flats. Themselves an outmoded
　　social concept. However. Do you know what that is . . . birds
　　with wrist watches?
BRON: Yes. Tripe.
HILARY: The Pathetic Fallacy. The idea that animals behave as
　　we do. Or feel at all. We have visitors.
BRON: Already?
HILARY: Other visitors. (*He is looking through the binoculars.*)
　　Your friend.
　　(HILARY *hands* BRON *the binoculars.* HILARY'S *movements should
　　now be swift and precise. Both are getting ready quickly,
　　removing any sign that they have been there very recently.*)
　　Were a person to cut across the field to the trees that person
　　could be seen instantly from the track.
BRON: I can't. I can't.
HILARY: Except if that person or persons were to wait until the
　　last moment when the car has come through the gate and is
　　coming round the back of the house there would be just
　　enough time to reach the wood before they came in. (*He
　　opens the drawer of the table and takes out a revolver.*) The car
　　has stopped by the gate. Eric is getting out to open it.

(HILARY *and* BRON *are now crouching down by the verandah steps. It ought to be tense and comic.*)

BRON: I like him.

HILARY: I like him.

BRON: She's all right.

HILARY: He's back in the car. She is a bleak bitch. They're just coming up to the corner. They are out of sight . . . NOW. (*They both dash down the verandah steps across the garden. Pause. Sound of a car door slamming, twice.*)

ERIC'S VOICE: Hello.

(ERIC *comes on. He is in his late twenties, a rather weak good looking young man. His wife* OLGA *is older, has a faint mid-European accent, plainly dressed. Ankle socks.*)

ERIC: Knock knock. Got a visitor.

(OLGA *comes on very slowly and stands waiting.*)

Don't say they're not here. No.

(OLGA *sees the rocking-chair is still faintly rocking. She looks at* ERIC. *He hasn't seen it. She stops it, without him noticing. She looks across the garden.*)

The car's here. They can't have gone far.

OLGA: What do you want to do?

ERIC: I don't know. What do you want to do?

(*Pause.*)

These chairs are nice. I always liked these chairs.

OLGA: What do you want to do?

ERIC: I said they're nice chairs. Do you like them? The chairs. Yes or no?

OLGA: Why?

(OLGA *sits down.* ERIC *gets up and looks in one of the rooms offstage.*)

ERIC: (*Off*) Our place isn't like this?

OLGA: You don't have any books.

ERIC: Besides books. The things. Bits of wood. Things they find on walks. Pebbles. Bits of glass. Bones. (*He walks round touching objects, looking at books, meddling.*)

OLGA: The contents of a schoolboy's pocket.

ERIC: Treasures.

OLGA: We pick flowers.

16

ERIC: Bluebells! Kids pick flowers. That's nothing. She picks weeds. That's art. I could have done art. It was an option. Art or mechanical drawing. Trigonometry. You never hear of that now. Not that it was ever big news.

OLGA: We could call coming back.

ERIC: Who else do I see? I like them. Why don't you go on?

OLGA: What happens to your picnic?

ERIC: *My* picnic is it now? It was you that suggested it.

OLGA: You wanted to go. You behave like a child. We could wait all day. They are not here. Come on.

ERIC: No.

OLGA: Why?

ERIC: What's wrong with just sitting. I like just sitting. I had two years on and off just sitting. Looking out. Allotments. Trucks shunted past. My personal piece of sky. Heaven.
(*Pause.*)
What could you see?

OLGA: Where?

ERIC: In prison, *dear*. Stir. The nick.

OLGA: If I looked, I could see a wall.

ERIC: That all? A wall?

OLGA: That, or the eye in the door. I forget. You should forget. Your little memories. Gosport. Wakefield. Your would-be souvenirs. They all have to be carried. So leave them. They are not important.

ERIC: That was always the refrain. 'It is not important.' 'Do not worry about it.' The box in the wardrobe, the pit in the floor. The ritual with the bathroom curtains. 'What are you doing?' 'It is not important.' 'Where are you going?' 'Never mind.'
(*The telephone rings.* ERIC *waits a moment then goes to answer it.*)

OLGA: No.

ERIC: You then.

OLGA: No.

ERIC: Why not?

OLGA: What is it to do with us? Leave it.
(ERIC *sits down and it stops ringing. There is a moment of relief, then it starts to ring again.* HILARY *comes in rapidly, revolver in*

17

hand. He ignores them and goes through into the inner room where the telephone is ringing. As he answers it, it stops. He comes back.)

HILARY: Sorry.

ERIC: We weren't sure what to do.

HILARY: Well. You have a telephone. Sometimes it rings. It seems to me then that you have a very limited number of choices. I mean, I have been known not to answer the door were someone to call unexpectedly for instance, but I always answer the telephone. You didn't telephone?

ERIC: We just called on the off-chance. Only you were out.

HILARY: Exercise, Eric. Stretching the old legs. Fleeing the spectre of coronary thrombosis.

OLGA: In your carpet slippers?

HILARY: My brogues are at the menders.

ERIC: Why the gun?

HILARY: I have been defending Elgar.

(*Enter* BRON, *breathless, with some grasses.*)

BRON: Visitors! Eric! Goodness! Isn't this a surprise. (*She kisses* ERIC *on both cheeks.*) And Olga. Well! Well! (*She shakes hands with* OLGA.) Was it anybody?

HILARY: It was a reverse charges call. A Mr Joseph Stalin is telephoning you from a Haslemere call box and wishes you to pay for the call. Will you accept the charge?
(HILARY *is restless, sensing there is something wrong with the room, something out of place. He roams round until he has located the* (*say*) *two objects* ERIC *has* (*very slightly*) *displaced.*)
This place is upside down.

BRON: Eric, some lemonade?

ERIC: I'll come.

BRON: Stay and entertain Hilary. Olga, you don't, do you?
(BRON *goes out.*)

HILARY: A lesson to us all. You don't drink. I'm not sure I've ever known you eat. Does she eat, Eric?

ERIC: Yes. We're just going on a picnic.

OLGA: Sandwiches in the woods, only.

ERIC: Well, a *picnic*.

HILARY: The most I've ever seen you have is a few sips of water.

And that was after a three-hour meeting when us lesser mortals adjourned for lunch. But not your good lady, Eric. She pours herself half a glass of very old water and keeps at it right through the afternoon.

ERIC: We thought we'd try out one of these specially designated picnic areas. In the forest by the lake. It's all laid out, apparently. There are big tree stumps for tables and little tree stumps for chairs.

HILARY: I may be sticking my neck out on this one, but that sounds as if somebody in authority's been using their imagination.

ERIC: Boats, toilets, music. And it all blends in. What we wondered . . . I suggested . . . if it would be a good idea if . . .

HILARY: We made up a foursome, you mean? That's a thought. So far as I know we've nothing on the agenda for today and in principle it sounds a fine idea. Still I'd better put it to the management. Don't want to take a unilateral decision on this one. (*He adjusts something else.*) This room looks as if it's been hit by an earthquake. What's been going on?

(*Enter* BRON.)

Bron. Mate o' mine. It appears our young friends are picnic-bound and we oldsters are more than welcome to tag along. What say? We've nothing scheduled have we?

BRON: Stop being silly. You know we've got people.

(HILARY *smacks his forehead in a gesture of absentmindedness.*)

HILARY: Dolt! Cretin! *Deceiver!* My sister Veronica is coming to lunch. Big occasion. The fatted calf. All the trimmings. And not only my sister but her newly knighted husband.

ERIC: Never mind.

HILARY: Always the way. Days, weeks go by and nothing doing then treat jostles with treat.

ERIC: There'll be other times.

BRON: Perhaps you and I could go on one of our little expeditions during the week.

HILARY: Hear that, Olga? Little plots being hatched behind the backs of the workers.

OLGA: You will be pleased to see your relatives?

BRON: Oh yes. Particularly Veronica. Her husband's a bit of a stick, but we're quite fond of him.

HILARY: What's that, dear?

BRON: Duff.

HILARY: I don't think you'd like him, Olga. Duff, basically, is just a nasty green bogey drizzling from the nose of art. However.

OLGA: Is she older or younger than you?

BRON: Younger.

HILARY: Older. No Eric I don't think I'd want to be on the roads today. Today is one of those days when the people, God bless them, will be out in force.

BRON: Why not?

HILARY: Well to be quite candid because one sees quite enough of them during the week. Come the weekend . . . and I know this isn't everybody's cup of tea . . . come the weekend I like to get right away from my fellow man, plonk the old backside down in a field somewhere, get my back up against a haystack, close my eyes and sit there while the skylarks and the thrushes and the bees etc. do their worst and Dame Nature weaves her healing magic. That's how I recharge my batteries. You can keep your leisure centres, your Costa Brava . . .

BRON: Chuck it.

HILARY: You can help us here, Olga. Before your somewhat adventitious arrival we were talking, my wife and I, about the alternative locations for this landscape.
(*Pause.*)
Say you had no means of knowing whereabouts you were, where would you say this was. Eric? A synonymous place. You are to imagine you have been put on a train, Olga, your destination something of a mystery. The train travels day and night for the best part of a week, finally is shunted into a siding. You try and see out. It is the middle of the night. Lights nearby. Loudspeakers. At dawn the doors are slid back and you fall out on to the platform, look round and see. . . (*He lifts his arms.*) this.
(*Pause.*)
Where would you say you were? Because I would have said Aldershot. Or if not Aldershot exactly, Pirbright. You have the pines.

BRON: Spruce in fact.

HILARY: Sandy soil. Scrub. Bracken. The odd silver birch. It's the common at Pirbright as seen from the Salisbury train. Or half a dozen places in Hampshire.

BRON: Pirbright's in Surrey.

HILARY: Aldershot then. Were you ever in Aldershot?

OLGA: No.

ERIC: Yes we were. We had a Chinese meal there one Sunday afternoon.

HILARY: That sounds as if it could be Aldershot. However, I'm afraid I must love you and leave you. We working girls. Olga, nice to see you in mufti, as it were. Eric be good. And Bronnie, don't keep them too long or they may not get a tree stump. (*He is going.*)

BRON: Hilary.

HILARY: What?

BRON: Take that thing with you. (*She points at the revolver.*)

HILARY: No. Put it back where it belongs. It lives in the drawer. (*He goes.*)

OLGA: Your husband does not like me.

ERIC: Olga.

BRON: He likes his routine.

OLGA: He likes his routine. He does not like me.

ERIC: Olga.

OLGA: I embarrass you. It is in bad taste to say that. It is without irony. I make you uncomfortable.

ERIC: You don't even try. She doesn't try. Just be nice.

OLGA: Nice. Is that nice. The railway train? Was that nice?

BRON: Never mind . . .

ERIC: Let's talk about something else.

OLGA: I say your husband does not like me and you are embarrassed. Why?

(ERIC *groans.*)

ERIC: She was only trying to be nice. You should try to be nice.

OLGA: These little feelings do not matter. Nice. They belong to the past.

BRON: They do matter, don't they? Otherwise everybody ends up feeling terrible. I do.

ERIC: It's different for Olga. She's had a different upbringing.

OLGA: It is not my upbringing. I had no upbringing. Feelings like that, feelings about feelings. Putting yourself in another person's place. These are luxuries for which there is no time any more. Making people *feel* better. What is the point in that. It does not last.

ERIC: Then why bother to tell us? Why not leave us to get on with it?

OLGA: They are the most embarrassed nation in the world, the English. You cannot look each other in the face. Eric can scarcely look me in the face, my *husband*. Husbands embarrassed by wives, wives embarrassed by husbands. Children by parents. Is there anyone not embarrassed in England? The Queen perhaps. She is not embarrassed. With the rest it's 'I won't make you feel bad so long as you don't make me feel bad'. Then everybody is happy. That is the way it works. That is the social contract. Society is making each other feel better.

ERIC: We'd better go.

OLGA: No. Stay. You enjoy it here. Eric likes you. He says you are his only friend.

ERIC: Olga. Why *say* it?

OLGA: I say your husband does not like me and you are embarrassed. I say my husband likes you and he is embarrassed. I do not understand it. I will go and sit in the car.

ERIC: Yes.

BRON: No.

ERIC: Oh God.

OLGA: Do not hurry. We are not in the least pushed for time. I am not hurt. (*She goes.*)

ERIC: Clumsy cow. I don't talk about you. Not all the time. I . . .

BRON: It doesn't *matter*. It's not important.

(*Pause.* ERIC *wanders round touching things again. Picking up items.*)

ERIC: I wish I read. I want to.

BRON: What's stopping you? Take something. He won't mind.

ERIC: No point.

BRON: Then you don't want to read, do you? You just want to want to.

ERIC: No.

BRON: It's like me. I used to think I wanted to leave Hilary. Then I realised I didn't want to. I just wanted to want to.
(*Pause.*)

ERIC: I tell you about Joyce? My sister.

BRON: Joyce. No. Why?

ERIC: I had a letter. She's going in for one of these child care officers. I reckon she's quite brave to be branching out. Thirty-eight.

BRON: Is that the one in Leicester?

ERIC: Nottingham.

BRON: The one who's married to the personnel officer.

ERIC: Labour relations.

BRON: That should be interesting.

ERIC: Apparently local government now you can't go wrong. They're on a sliding scale. Haven't *you* any news?
(BRON *is still staring after* OLGA.)
Leave her.

BRON: Hilary's father's in the bin again.

ERIC: Is that bad?

BRON: Belsize Park.

ERIC: They're generally on the outskirts somewhere.

BRON: What?

ERIC: Homes.

BRON: Belsize Park is London.

ERIC: Belsize Park? It sounds like a country house.

BRON: I suppose it was once. Robin's come out of the army.

ERIC: He the good-looking one?

BRON: He doesn't know what he wants to do. He wondered about starting a safari park. He's got someone to put up the money but I think they may be going out now, safari parks. What do you think?

ERIC: I've only been to one and the animals were all asleep. It's the same as a cage only bigger: they'll soon know it inside out.

BRON: Zoos seem to be full of people staring at animals that hail from the same countries as they do. Africans, Japanese. It's as if they've gone to the zoo because it's where they're sure to find a familiar face. Friends who just happen to be living abroad.

ERIC: Japan doesn't have any special animals though, does it?

BRON: Doesn't it? I don't know.

ERIC: I wish I could see them.

BRON: Who?

ERIC: Your visitors. I wouldn't talk. I wouldn't show you up.

BRON: Eric.

ERIC: I'd keep out of sight.

BRON: Peep through the banisters.

ERIC: They've no need to see her.

BRON: You're all she's got.

ERIC: What're they like?

BRON: Not sure now. What are we like now? The same. Or even more the same. That's the difference.

ERIC: Maybe they could put a word in for me?

BRON: I wrote. You know I wrote.

ERIC: But maybe if I met them. She might like me. Feel sorry for me. You like me. I'm good at making people like me.

BRON: I'll see.

ERIC: So can I stay?

BRON: Eric. You shouldn't ask. It's family. It's not fair on them.

ERIC: Why? Because I'm just a draughtsman from Portsmouth Dockyard. The sort of people you're reduced to.

BRON: Eric. They're coming all this way to see us.

ERIC: Skip it. It will be boiling in the car because she won't have opened the windows. She won't even have noticed. It's not important. She sweats. There's no excuse for that, is there. Nowadays. I've told her. That's not important either. Because she once had it much worse nothing else counts. You'd think it might make her jump at all the little things. Perms, lipstick. Frocks. No. It's not important.

(HILARY *begins to play the piano offstage. It is the same hymn, 'Praise, my soul, the King of Heaven'*.)

Anyway, I'd better go for this picnic.

BRON: Stay a bit longer. Go on.

ERIC: I wish she was dead. I wish I could go out to the car now and find her dead. That would be a real picnic.

BRON: Eric.

(ERIC *goes as* HILARY *begins to sing the words of the hymn.*)

HILARY: (*Off*) 'Praise him for his grace and favour,
　　　　　To our fathers in distress.'

BRON: Hilary.

HILARY: (*Off*) 'Praise Him still the same as ever,
　　　　　Slow to chide and . . .'

BRON: *Hilary.*

(HILARY *stops and comes on.*)

What gives you the right to be so bloody condescending?

HILARY: Did you know they've scrapped the Holy Communion? They're experimenting with something called Series 1, Series 2 and Series 3. That doesn't sound like the Eucharist to me. That sounds like baseball.

BRON: Who are we?

HILARY: I am a snob. We know that.

BRON: He likes you.

HILARY: I imagine when it comes to the next prayer book they won't write He, meaning Him with a capital H. God will be written in the lower case to banish any lurking sense of inferiority his worshippers might feel.

(*Pause.*)

The C. of E. was my first love. Until the age of sixteen I had every intention of going into the ministry.

BRON: Saved everybody a lot of trouble if you had.

HILARY: Had I chosen orders I would have been a bishop by now.

BRON: She's a lonely woman. What pass do you flip to allow you to behave like that?

HILARY: One of the few lessons I have learned in life is that there is invariably something odd about women who wear ankle socks. Olga. Four letters. Anagrams Gaol and Goal. Eric. Rice. A pale, flavourless substance consisting of millions of seemingly identical grains.

BRON: He's just a lost boy.

HILARY: This isn't Never Never Land.

BRON: You could pretend. For half an hour.

HILARY: I appreciate Olga has seen things she cannot forget. What is tiresome is that she will not let anyone else forget that she can't forget them. I get it every day at the office. They're a dismal couple and I see no reason why I should have them in my house.

BRON: Your house. This *shack*.

HILARY: My house. My country home. A doting frump with her silly little copper's nark of a husband. Who is he? A common criminal. What is she? A woman to whom the past is simply misery and horror. Not surprising she can't wait to get to the future. We have nothing in common at all.

BRON: (*Without emotion*) Except the one thing. You're all traitors. (HILARY *goes and puts a record on the turntable and comes back. The next speech is over the slow introduction to a very grand Strauss waltz.*)

HILARY: Considering this taunt was quite deserved and in substance true, he thought he kept his temper very well. The easiest accusations to bear are, after all, the ones of which one is innocent. To be accused of something of which one is guilty, that is the intolerable thing. Though I use guilt to mean responsibility. Not guilt. However.

BRON: Your whole life is on the other side of the glass. And there is nobody watching.

HILARY: If the past is anything to go by, we would normally sulk for the rest of the day. Then towards evening we'd make it up, get drunk and dance. But we haven't all day and we can't get drunk until the company comes so . . . come on, old lady.

(HILARY *and* BRON *dance immaculately, in best ballroom fashion. Occasionally he shouts instructions or the time.* 'Two, three and turn. Two three and reverse.'
He is also very easily puffed and almost has to stop and fight for breath, but goes on.
BRON *stops suddenly. Listens. Goes to the gramophone and stops it. Listens again.*
There is the sound of a car door. Voices off.)

BRON: I am terrified.

(*They wait.*

VERONICA, *a slim, very chic lady comes on slowly, picking her*
way with a fixed smile, not sure whether she's come to the right
place. DUFF, *her somewhat stouter husband, bringing up the*
rear.)

VERONICA: Bron! Oh Bronnie, darling! Hugs, darling. Hugs,
hugs, hugs. Such hugs.

BRON: You found us, then?

VERONICA: And Hilary. Hilary. You look *well*. Doesn't he look
well?

BRON: Dear Duff!

(DUFF *kisses* BRON.)

VERONICA: So trim. And so young.

(HILARY *holds out his hand.*)

DUFF: Put that careful hand away. We too shall kiss. And kiss
properly. See, Veronica, the great man blushes. My dear, it
is accepted now. Men can kiss. And remain men.

HILARY: No, they kiss here too. No . . . I . . . we are very happy to
see you.

BRON: Oh yes. *Yes.*

HILARY: Welcome to the Forest of Arden.

(*A slightly awkward pause.*)

VERONICA: This is heaven, Bron. Do admit. A Wendy House. And
here you both are. Looking so young. Children.

HILARY: You found it all right?

DUFF: We came in an embassy car. They seemed to know exactly
where it was.

HILARY: That's not surprising.

VERONICA: Darling. Is there somewhere I could wash my hands?

BRON: You want to 'freshen up'. Then let me show you 'the
geography of the house.'

(*They laugh.*)

Oh the heaven of jokes. That's our little garden.

VERONICA: Sweet. Duff. Look. The garden.

DUFF: The English garden.

BRON: We'll go through.

VERONICA: (*Off*) So cool here. Moscow was *boiling*.

DUFF: You live here in the summer? Charming.

HILARY: It's hardly Hookham.

DUFF: Your books. A garden. Some distant prospect. Dieser kleine Pavillon. Paradise. How very clever of you. (*He mouths.*) Are we overheard?

HILARY: Sorry?

(DUFF *mimes someone listening.*)

Here? No. Why, what do you want to say?

DUFF: Nothing. Nothing. *Nothing.* Anyway, Hookham is now a diocesan conference centre. It's wild with bishops.

HILARY: So I'm told.

DUFF: They've put in a sauna bath. What do bishops want with a sauna bath? You look *so* well.

HILARY: Flourishing. Flourishing.

DUFF: Thoreau. A second Walden. The great, good place. How enviable. Listen to that silence! Delicious.

HILARY: What are you lecturing about?

DUFF: Lecturing, lecturing? Lecturing?

HILARY: I thought you were in Moscow to give a lecture?

DUFF: Oh *lecturing*! Forster. Forster. For my sins. And for my supper. For my sins and for my supper.

HILARY: He died, I gather. Forster.

DUFF: I rather think so, yes. Yes, he's gone at last. That mild but steady glow put out. I was at the funeral. But not *Passage. To India.* My lecture. Not the evils, say rather the indignities of colonialism. That is what they are expecting but no. *Howards End.* I shall run up the flag of personal relations for ever and ever. That should set the cat among the pigeons. Beard the Wilcox in his den, be it Stock Exchange or Palace of Culture.

HILARY: That's bold. I've got a first edition of it somewhere.

(*Begins to look.*) I'm not sure it's not inscribed.

DUFF: Only connect, comrades. Only connect.

HILARY: I never quite understood what that meant.

DUFF: Neither did I. But it is not important. It's all the things it might mean, the penumbra of half meanings, the nimbus of uncertainty. That's its power.

HILARY: I don't know what it means at all.

DUFF: What do all such enjoinders mean? 'Grace under pressure.' 'Be generous and delicate and pursue the prize.' 'Only

28

connect.' Forster. Hemingway. Henry James. All add up to the same thing. Be nice. Behave, or people won't like you. Neo-platonism diluted. The farewell at the mouth of the cave. Remember, be nice!

(HILARY *finds a copy and hands it to* DUFF *who looks at it.*)

HILARY: Cambridge.

DUFF: Cambridge. Love. Life.

HILARY: I was waiting for you to admire our trees.

DUFF: Yes. Yes. I do.

HILARY: Spruce, apparently.

DUFF: Indeed? And what happens beyond the trees?

HILARY: 'Beyond the wild wood comes the wide world.'

DUFF: The freedom of the fields, the shelter of the woods. Un vrai paysage moralisé.

HILARY: I must apologise for the birds. They do not do their stint so far as singing is concerned. When you consider most of them are only here for the summer, that winter finds them in Bournemouth, or even Amersham, it really is rather unfair. *I'd* sing.

DUFF: You're not happy?

HILARY: Did I say that?

DUFF: Are you happy?

HILARY: Well, Duff, shall I put it like this. I'm not sorry it's not Surrey.

DUFF: Yes. I see. The real tragedy with us lately has been the loss of the elm. Practically every single elm has gone.

HILARY: Does that make a difference?

DUFF: A vast difference. We are only now starting to count the cost. Wiltshire is a wilderness. A spokesman in the Department was telling me that upwards of nine million trees have perished. One of the most characteristic elements of the English landscape cancelled out. A gap in nature. Constable. Cotman, Crome now documents. Invaluable evidence of the countryside as it was ten, even five years ago. The loss of an inheritance.
'Felled, felled, all felled.
After comers cannot guess the beauty been.'

HILARY: I'm sorry.

29

DUFF: 'Nous n'irons plus au bois. Les lauriers sont coupés.'

HILARY: I wonder what those girls can be up to?

DUFF: It is sad to find oneself so often striking the elegiac note when one is by temperament and inclination a modernist. One's whole nature yearns towards the new yet time and time again one finds oneself averting one's eyes from evidences of modernity. Pain. Pain. Too much pain. One thinks of Bath. Northampton. Leeds. Worcester. I too am an exile, and in my own country. From my own time. You should see Glasgow, that Grecian place. Edinburgh. And dear, dear Brighton. How much better off you are, Hilary. Amputated. Cut clean. Not to see the slow death of friends. And as the monuments, so I fear the institutions.

HILARY: Yes. I was reading the other day that Lyons were closing down the teashops. That does seem to me to be scandalous. Where will people go?

DUFF: I don't know. I do not know. You must be rubbing your hands.

HILARY: At the death of the teashop? No.

DUFF: All part of the prescribed withering away. Only what you've been telling us to expect.

HILARY: Me, Duff?

DUFF: History delivering the goods.

HILARY: Not me.

DUFF: Your team.

HILARY: On the contrary the nice thing about my people . . . how quaint to call them a team . . . is that they're very old-fashioned. Not at all forward looking. And whatever their shortcomings in point of the liberty of the subject very litter-conscious. Do I want the old place to change? I don't think so. I have left it. It must stay the same or there is no point in having come away. I certainly don't want things to improve. Though I remain, of course, firmly in two minds. Whereas ideologically I must count every sign of decay an improvement, so my personal inclination is to think of every improvement as decay. Certainly where the end of Lyons is concerned. Was that presented as an improvement? I imagine so.

DUFF: I forget. But it is paradoxical that it is the socialist regimes which are so bent on demolishing the institutions of the past that are the most scrupulous guardians of its monuments. One thinks of Dresden, doesn't one (every stone restored) Die Altstaddte: Prague, Warsaw. A hint of aspic. But does that matter? They remain. They survive.

HILARY: Moscow, you can take tea on every street corner.

DUFF: The fact is, at this moment in our history I fear we flounder. And if one were asked, as indeed all too often one is asked (conferences, think-tanks, round-ups at the year's end) the inevitable question: 'Diagnose our predicament' 'Sort out some symptoms' 'Pin-point the problem' 'Name the culprit' (Ah ha!) In a word 'What's Up?' Then lamely I say that in the people I come into contact with . . . last week in Wiltshire, man laying us new cobbles, a genuine craftsman, stalwart figure (minded of Hardy) thirty-five, two children, set up on his own, £90 a week, doing very nicely thank you . . . *and no bad barometer* . . . in such people again and again one comes on this settled conviction that *things will turn out all right in the end*. And this conviction, this *common* sense not so different from the official philosophy here that, leave history to itself and one way or another all the eggs are going to end up in you basket.

(*While* DUFF *has been talking he has been going round the room, looking at books, picking up objects and replacing them.*)

HILARY: (*Pause*) What I think I would say, Duff, is this: people are the same the world over.

DUFF: (*Sagely*) Absolutely.

(HILARY *rights the books and objects* DUFF *has disturbed.*)

HILARY: Of course the service is bad here. But then it always has been. Apparently one waited an age in a restaurant even under the Tsars. Nothing has changed.

DUFF: Quite. And do we differ? Not fundamentally. Because slow lane, fast lane, we all of us seem to be headed in the same direction. Where? Well, in the general direction of the millennium. But remember, no goals or grand arrivals. No end in sight. No fullness of time. Just dribbling along. Stop, go. Carriages in a siding. Shunted along, middle of the night.

Where are we? Never mind. We're en route for the millennium. Not that we'll see it. The millennium's a place to go to not arrive at. Millenniums mean murder. Trials in football stadiums. Babies on bayonets and poets in prison, indignities offered ambassadors' wives. No. Amelioration. Improvement. As here. Not the best. Too soon for the best. Slow but sure. Slow but share. World wide amelioration. (*He winces.*) I'm being bitten.

HILARY: Really? It's funny, they don't bite me.

(*Enter* VERONICA *and* BRON, *giggling.*)

VERONICA: I'm just saying to Bronnie one of the delights of Moscow is that young men keep sidling up to Duff and saying 'Have you any jeans'? I mean Duff! Jeans! I shriek.

DUFF: In point of fact, Veronica, I have a pair of jeans.

VERONICA: Never. Oh yes, you do. They're a sort of tinned salmon colour. He bought them at Simpsons for when he does Saturday shopping down St John's Wood High Street.

DUFF: I'm not a complete fool, you know.

VERONICA: Listen, I haven't given you your stocking. (*She gets a bag.*)

HILARY: How's Father?

VERONICA: Pa? Marvellous. Tip-top. What's this? Oh, the garlic crusher. (Is that the sort you wanted?) Gentlemen's Relish.

BRON: Heaven. Two pots.

VERONICA: Your hymns record. King's College Chapel.

BRON: Oh God.

VERONICA: Crossword puzzles.

BRON: Bath Olivers.

VERONICA: The last Anthony Powell.

DUFF: I'm told it's very good. I think he's probably brought it off.

VERONICA: A *Times*.

HILARY: I see that at work.

VERONICA: No, Pa is marvellous. Never better. Can't see him pegging out for years yet. He thrives.

HILARY: He always does in the bin. Ordering everybody about. It's like old times.

VERONICA: Like, duck? It *is*. He's so confused. He thinks Ma is still alive, Duncan and Frank. Gussie with her bugle. Dozens

32

from the trenches. All there. It's just like a wonderful cocktail party. No distinction of age, creed or class. Everybody.

HILARY: The resurrection.

BRON: The open society.

DUFF: It's actually a form of arteriosclerosis.

HILARY: Now, how about a drop of the old nail varnish?

VERONICA: Whisky for me. I won't venture to say Scotch.

HILARY: Duff?

DUFF: Not for me.

HILARY: Oh.

DUFF: With the meal perhaps. Now, no.

HILARY: Duff tells me Lyons have closed all their tea shops.

DUFF: I didn't tell you. You told me.

HILARY: Where on earth do you go for a cup of tea now?

VERONICA: One seems to manage.

HILARY: The nice thing about Lyons was that they cropped up at such regular intervals. Rather like lavatories in that respect. I suppose one could have spent the day hopping from Lyons to lav and lav to Lyons all the way across London. If one was so minded. But not any more. However. They still have lavs?

DUFF: Yes.

HILARY: That's a relief.

BRON: Here they're in rather short supply. One does tend to see people doing it in corners.

HILARY: Only if you look. She looks.

VERONICA: I saw somebody peeing in Jermyn Street the other day. I thought, Is this the end of civilisation as we know it. Or is it simply somebody peeing in Jermyn Street?

HILARY: And did you come to any decision on that?

VERONICA: No. But I saw a rat in St James's the next day. That seemed somehow an omen. These things add up.

DUFF: Well! Here we are. A country house. Wine. Talk. Friends.

VERONICA: Summer days.

DUFF: They seem to persist. Country houses. By dint of the turnstile. We open our gardens twice a year.

VERONICA: Rhododendrons are our strong suit. A riot of colour.

HILARY: No kangaroos?

DUFF: Staff are prohibitive. Still, open prisons, homes for the aged, management training centres . . . museums or menageries they survive.

HILARY: They must. The Big House as nutshell, the novelist's venue. Lose that and what happens to the detective story? On the sunlit lawn the empty rug, the open book and the faintly rocking chair compose a setting from which someone has suddenly departed, leaving a thriller open at the point where on a sunlit lawn the empty rug and the open book and the chair faintly rocking indicate someone has suddenly departed.

BRON: (*Quickly*) We haven't congratulated you.

DUFF: What on?

BRON: *Sir* Hector.

DUFF: Hardly a surprise. One's definite due.

VERONICA: If you ask me, it's just a sharp nudge in the direction of the grave.

HILARY: Well done thou good and faithful servant.

DUFF: Nobody more so. They search the ranks for someone still fit for hard labour and I curse my stature that singles me out. Oh let me not be named, I think, when some fresh commission is mooted. Not me. Then comes the call. You, sir! Fall out! So chained and marched away. Another sentence to run concurrently with the others. Another room to sit in all those slow afternoons. Carafe and tumbler, blotter and sharpened pencils . . . the instruments of my martyrdom. Still, it is what I have to do. Ich kann nicht anders. But pity me. (*He raises his hands in a gesture of martyrdom and blessing.*) Pity my poor prickling piles. I am unfree. A slave. I am a servant at Liberty Hall.

VERONICA: What exactly do you do, darling? Or should I know better than to ask? Except you always knew better than to tell me.

HILARY: Very dull. I have an office. I translate. My advice is occasionally asked and ignored. Not very different from the Foreign Office. However. Why is working for the party like a mushroom?

VERONICA: Why?

HILARY: Because you're kept in the dark and every so often someone comes and throws a bucket of shit over you.

VERONICA: Actually I'd heard that, only in my version it was the BBC.

HILARY: What are you writing down?

DUFF: I want to . . . just make a note of that . . . joke . . . I never remember jokes. Excellent memory for facts. But jokes just do not seem to stick. Why is that? Mushroom was it? And of course one does need them. Jokes. Very handy with the young. One must count oneself fortunate in numbering among one's acquaintance several Young People, whose intellectual and spiritual restlessness I find salutary. I come away refreshed. Invigorated. And they in their turn, feel that the world of decisions has a human face if only because they see it over a glass of beer.

VERONICA: Beer!

DUFF: The place where I find these contacts stand me in unexpectedly good stead is in Whitehall, of all places. Dans les coulisses. Royal Commissions, Arts Council, grant allocations and so on. One can be sitting there with a group of well-disposed people . . . intelligent, informed and above all *concerned*. The suggestion is that such and such a proposal will benefit young people. But will it benefit Stephen, the hospital porter? How will Trevor, a counter assistant at Dickins and Jones, fit into the scheme or Fiona, his girlfriend? And I'm afraid the answer I come up with is often very different from that of my esteemed colleagues. The result is I'm getting a name as a bit of a maverick. Duff, they say, Duff is being *difficile*. But I must live with that. What I think is vitally important is not to let the young assume that middle age must necessarily mean the middle ground. There can still be jokes. Adventures. Irreverence. (*To himself as he writes.*) A bucket of shit. Good. Good.

BRON: We don't see many young people.

HILARY: Eric? Olga? Called only this morning, wanting us to bathe. We can bathe. Or stroll in these commodious woods. Tea under the trees. Every facility.

35

VERONICA: People call? Here?

HILARY: All the time.

BRON: They're a sad couple. He was the clerk in the dockyard at Portsmouth, though she was the real brains. When they swapped her she insisted on him being part of the package. Rather touching. I should feel very Hampstead bathing now. The Ladies Pond. My bathing days are done.

HILARY: Do old gentlemen still hurl themselves into the Serpentine on Boxing Day?

VERONICA: No. That went out with Pathé News.

DUFF: As I understand it, bathing is now considered distinctly therapeutic. We've got some of our chronic arthritis people into the baths at the Middlesex Hospital and they go splashing around like two-year-olds.

(HILARY *takes the revolver out of the drawer.*)

HILARY: Best bathing I ever had was in the war. North Africa. (*He takes aim at something across the verandah on the edge of the garden.*) Did you ever fly in a Sunderland? The old flying boats. (Don't move, sweetheart. That's beautiful.) Flew from Gibraltar to Crete in one once, during the war. (Head up a fraction.) Came down in the drink just off the coast of Tripoli. Engine trouble. (To your right a bit, darling.)

BRON: Oh, leave it, Hilary, leave it.

HILARY: Shut up. We sat on top of the water, opposite a brilliant white shore.

(DUFF *has been getting quite nervous and stands up.*)

Sit down, man, for God's sake.

(*He puts the gun down.*) Bugger. We just slipped down into the sea and swam ashore. It was perfect.

VERONICA: The Mediterranean? Not any more, dear. It's the Elsan of Europe. And we tried Tripoli two years ago. It's the Costa del Tesco.

DUFF: The image of soldiers bathing has a long history in art. Does Berenson have an essay on that? Those armed and flexed for war, now relaxed, vulnerable. At rest.

HILARY: It's my opinion, for what it's worth, that Berenson was a bit of an arsehole. Don't you agree?

36

DUFF: Oh . . . yes. On balance, I think, probably, yes.

HILARY: An ancient American arsehole that anybody who was anybody had to stop and lick if they happened to be passing through Florence. Did you ever go?

DUFF: I believe we may have called once – purely out of politeness.

HILARY: I didn't. I wasn't famous enough then. I could go now, of course, if he were alive. Now that I'm something of a celebrity. Instead people come and see me. Berenson at I Tatti, Max at Rapallo, Willie at Cap Ferrat. Me here.

BRON: Except you're not an artist.

HILARY: And always in the background some capable lady of either sex, tucking in the rugs, censuring his utterance, presenting the old boy to the world. Protecting him. Rationing him. The great man. Life is short. Art is long. Breakfast is prompt at eight o'clock.

(HILARY *suddenly brings up the revolver and fires. It should not be a loud noise. One of those long revolvers fitted with a silencer.*

BRON *goes.*)

Jolly good.

This is when I miss Shep. (*He goes.*)

VERONICA: Help! Help! Help!

DUFF: Nonsense. Running pretty true to form. Tiresome, but not more so than one remembered. Nice books. (*He wanders round the room, absorbed in its contents.*)

VERONICA: They're both so old. Aren't they?

DUFF: Oh *very* nice. I thought Bron was looking a bit desseché.

VERONICA: She had a little cry upstairs.

DUFF: Such a slum. What about?

VERONICA: What about? The Scotch for a start. It's Jeyes Fluid. I would go mad. All this unnecessary countryside.

DUFF: It's true he was never overly rustic.

VERONICA: She'd come back like a shot. Have you said anything to him?

DUFF: Pretty. Very pretty. Wasted here.

VERONICA: The old fraud.

DUFF: And mostly first editions. You think he's being lazy, it's then he's working hardest. Suspect him and his fidelity will put you to shame. Trust him and he instantly betrays you. What sort of man is that?

VERONICA: Lyons! He never went into Lyons in his life.

DUFF: Are you sure?

VERONICA: I am his sister. And what about that gun?

DUFF: That's all silly. So silly. Still he seems not to go at the drink now.

VERONICA: I've been waiting for someone to say that about Berenson for years.

DUFF: It was actually a very ill-informed remark. Berenson was art-historian first and sage second. He didn't seek society. Society sought him. His exile was not less fruitful for being populous. Whereas who comes here?

VERONICA: You, for one. Look out. Home is the hunter!

(HILARY *enters with a dead hare, which he holds up by the ears.*)

HILARY: Isn't he a beauty! Take him. Go on.

DUFF: No.

HILARY: Why? He's dead.

DUFF: I know he's dead.

VERONICA: Darling, it's only a rabbit.

HILARY: It's not. It's a hare.

VERONICA: I've always thought hares were simply rabbits writ large.

HILARY: Not at all. They're quite far apart in the evolutionary chain. Further apart than a dog and a fox for instance, which are likewise deceptively similar. Rabbits are gregarious, slow-moving, leading a rich, underground life. Hares are swift, solitary, creatures of the open field. (*He waves the hare at Duff.*)

DUFF: NO!

VERONICA: Hilary, behave! Acting the fool!

DUFF: There's blood on my face.

VERONICA: It's only the tiniest spot. Oh and another bit here.

HILARY: Sorry. Sorry. Should I apologise to Duff?

DUFF: Don't be absurd.

VERONICA: Yes.

HILARY: Duff. I apologise.

VERONICA: I should think so too. There. All gone. What are we having for lunch?

HILARY: Rabbit.

DUFF: Not this one?

HILARY: Duff, how many more times? This is a hare. We shall have to hang you a while, won't we?

BRON: (*Voice off*) Food!

DUFF: We've had a big best seller about rabbits. Good rabbits and bad rabbits. I haven't got round to it yet. I suspect the presence of allegory, which is always a slight deterrent. Shall I stagger in? Rabbits are coming back in England now. (*He goes.*) Myxomatosis or no myxomatosis.

(HILARY *goes off with* DUFF *carrying his record.* VERONICA *remains, smoking.*

HILARY *returns as a hymn begins on the gramophone.*)

HILARY: One advantage of living in Russia is that it's one of the few places where smoking doesn't cause cancer. At least the authorities don't say it does, so one must presume it doesn't.

VERONICA: Are you happy?

HILARY: Why does everybody keep asking me that? No. I'm not happy. But I'm not un-happy about it. However.

(VERONICA *goes.*

HILARY *lifts the hare to show it to the watcher in the garden.*) Rather good, don't you think. Just bagged him. Bonny creatures. Still. One has to live. Popping in for a spot of lunch now. Old friends from way back. Broach a few bottles of the old vino rosso, have a natter about old times. Cheers.

(HILARY *goes off, the music continuing, as* BRON *enters with a tray. She lifts it high to show it to whoever is watching in the garden and just before she does so the music cuts out as* HILARY *takes the record off inside the house.* BRON *puts the tray down on the top step of the verandah and goes off.*)

CURTAIN

ACT TWO

BRON *and* VERONICA *are talking. It is after lunch.*

VERONICA: Such a pretty garden. Such a pretty house.

BRON: We love it.

VERONICA: It is a knack. Making the place cosy. Newport Street was cosy. Tiny, but cosy.

BRON: We nest. The books help.

VERONICA: Ye-es.

BRON: And with the end of summer we walk out of here without even locking the door, come back next spring and nothing will have been touched. Where else in the world could you do that? (*She retrieves the tray with empty plate etc. from the top step of the verandah.*)

VERONICA: Wiltshire once. Not any more. There are muggers in Malmesbury.

BRON: The Hebrides, I suppose. Coll. Tiree. He keeps pretending this is Scotland.

VERONICA: Heavenly rabbit. Like chicken used to be before they started locking the poor loves up in factories. Do they have those here? Battery farms?

BRON: No.

VERONICA: How very sensible. You are lucky eating so simply. We would, but it's too complicated.

BRON: I miss shopping.

VERONICA: Don't. London is a midden. Every street knee deep in filth.

BRON: Moscow is clean.

VERONICA: Darling, spotless! Are those sweet peas?

BRON: Beans.

VERONICA: How clever. Clever old Bron.

40

BRON: You look younger.

VERONICA: To tell the truth, I did actually have a tiny op. Took up a bit of the slack. Why not? Free country.

BRON: All that couldn't happen quickly enough for me. Getting older. The stroke of fifty I was all set to turn into a wonderful woman. You know what I mean by a wonderful woman.

VERONICA: Yes. I'm married to one.

BRON: The wife to a doctor or a vicar's wife. Chairman of the County Council, a pillar of the W.I. A wise, witty, white-haired old lady, who's always stood on her own feet until one day at the age of eighty she comes out of the County Library and falls under the weight of her improving book, breaks her hip and dies, peacefully, continently and without fuss under a snowy coverlet in the cottage hospital. And coming away from her funeral in a country churchyard on a bright winter's afternoon people say, 'She was a wonderful woman.' That's what I wanted to be. Only here there's nobody to be it for.

VERONICA: Nobody to be it for anywhere nowadays.

BRON: I shall die and they'll still not be able to pronounce my name. Just a coffin waiting on the tarmac to go on the night flight to Heathrow.

VERONICA: I've a feeling they don't have cottage hospitals now. I'm not even sure about county councils. There was some alteration, Duff was on the commission. Which only leaves the W.I. and that's not what it was. Talks on abortion and new trends in foreplay.

BRON: But you need an audience. Character needs an audience or what are you? Here, who's watching?

VERONICA: Hilary.

BRON: Hilary. Hilary is watching Hilary. Watching Hilary.

VERONICA: As ever.

BRON: Slightly better if he were dead. Then I could come home and be his widow. So much more rewarding than being his wife. I wake in the middle of the night thinking: I know what this is: it's happily ever after.

VERONICA: It's not the place. Think of coming to in Wiltshire,

beached beside my chosen piece of matrimonial software.
Are we going to walk?

BRON: Do you like trees?

VERONICA: I don't mind.

BRON: There's this way. Or that way. East. West. Guermantes.
Combray. Either way, trees.

VERONICA: Yes. They have rather overdone it.

BRON: Each one the same height, the same distance from next.
Line after line after line.

VERONICA: Duff's taken up embroidery, did I tell you?

BRON: One day our first summer I took a picnic and went along
the edge of the trees meaning to reach the corner of the
plantation, see what was on the other side. I walked and walked,
all day and when I eventually gave up the trees still went on
in the same straight line. No break to the horizon. At any
point here you might be at any other point. Any time any
other time. The leaves don't fall. No spring. No autumn.
Nowhere.

VERONICA: Yes. Well, I wasn't frantic to go. These are hardly the
shoes.

BRON: The one other place I felt the same was Los Angeles.
(*Pause.*)

VERONICA: Say we were to lure you to London. Any thoughts?
Duff (Duff!) thinks it could be arranged. This is death.
Come back.

BRON: One gets used to it.

VERONICA: One gets used to it. I used to hate Walton Street until
it became all antique shops. Is he happy?

BRON: He never imagined he would have to join. Actually rub
shoulders. He thought he would carry his secret to the
grave.

VERONICA: The country churchyard. I don't believe it. He's just
a tease. He'd have had to tell somebody. That's the way all
good teases have to end. What fun. What wonderful lifelong
fun. I am not what you all think I am. Just like when one
was young and thought one had an inner life. Who's that
brute in the garden? Is he watching you or protecting you?

BRON: I don't know. I shouldn't think he knows. He's been

there all summer.

VERONICA: The liberty! I'd soon get shot of him.

BRON: I'm not sure I want to.

VERONICA: You should go straight out and say, 'Who is your immediate superior?' then get on the phone, and make a nuisance of yourself. I know it's different here, but it's not. Nag, nag, nag. Nag so much they realise it will be easier to do it than not. There is no other principle involved.

BRON: What totalitarian institutions have you dealt with?

VERONICA: The worst. The North Thames Gas Board. I'd shift him.

BRON: At least he's an audience. Watching me gardening, getting up in the morning. Hilary reading, feeding the birds. Like having a tortoise, you can't always spot it. Then you fall over him, asleep in the sun. I like it.

(HILARY *and* DUFF *come in.*)

HILARY: Did you ever come across Gaitskell?

DUFF: Many times.

HILARY: I only met him once. Nice man. We had a long conversation about . . . hamsters.

DUFF: Hamsters?

HILARY: Yes. Like what? You were saying you liked something.

BRON: Here. I like here.

DUFF: Charming. It's charming. It's a poem.

(*Pause.*)

I just want to plant the seed. Take the temperature of the water. That's all I want to do at this moment. That's all I'm empowered to do. I'm not looking for a Yes or a No. I just want to slot the suggestion in at the back of your mind, then we can go on from there. But know that the possibility exists. The door is at least ajar.

HILARY: Isn't that nice. So nice. Hear that, Bron. I think that's very . . . nice.

(*Pause.*)

Do you know what I've always wanted to do? *Desert Island Discs.*

DUFF: Well, why not? Why not? I am a governor of the Corporation. One word. The Chairman a personal friend.

Bowled over.

BRON: Elgar.

HILARY: Bron has never liked music.

BRON: I do like music. It's the appreciation of it I don't like.

DUFF: And . . . what is it . . . one book, apart from the Bible and Shakespeare.

HILARY: *The Book of Common Prayer*.

DUFF: Yes! Yes! The last thing anybody would expect.

BRON: Of course.

DUFF: I can't wait. The castaway. The castaway (I do not say prodigal) returned. Riveting.

HILARY: Returned? (*Pause*.) I couldn't record it here?

DUFF: No. I think you'll find it's a studio job. Portland Place.

HILARY: Portland Place.

DUFF: Tube to Oxford Circus.

HILARY: The other thought that's been running through my head (you'll laugh at me now) is, 'Come on, Hilary, old boy. I know it's a bit late in the day but why don't you pull the old socks up and do what you've always wanted to do, deep down, namely, have a stab at Art.'

DUFF: I don't believe it. Veronica. I do not believe it. On the plane. Did I not say?

VERONICA: Pa does pretty paintings.

DUFF: We are talking of literature, Veronica, not therapy.

HILARY: Art. The ineffable. The role of redeemer. Become an order out of chaos merchant. Novels, poems. A play.

DUFF: I could place your memoirs tomorrow.

HILARY: Telling it all has become so respectable. Dirt. Treachery. Murder. Boys. My dear, who cares?

DUFF: Oh no. Boys are nothing nowadays. And memoirs make a mint.

HILARY: Always at the head of the charts. Always at No 1 American Express, Diners Club. Art trumps them all. It's the other country. Betray anything for that. But not memoirs, quite.

DUFF: No? Art is memory.

VERONICA: Down, Proust!

HILARY: I can't see yet how far from one's life one has to stand to make it art. You know? At what angle. It's not enough to tell the tale. One's private predicament. One man running naked through Europe.

DUFF: From a purely commercial point of view almost anything would have a ready sale. Except perhaps poetry. Poetry might be taken to indicate a certain weakening of the intellect.

HILARY: Yes. A faint message in morse indicating the ship is sinking. No. It wants to be something more substantial than that. My testament. An edifice standing four square against the winds of dogma. Light streaming from every window. A mansion to which all my life has simply been the drive.

VERONICA: Or the garden path.

HILARY: Is that the way to redeem myself? What do you say, Bron?

BRON: Why not? It's where it's all supposed to make sense, isn't it. Death, disappointment. The joyful serenity of Mozart. Wagner's ineffable majesty. Art. I should stick to religion. At least that has no pretensions to immortality any more.

HILARY: My wife.

BRON: He's not serious, you know. You don't think he's being serious? He doesn't mean a word he says.

HILARY: In England we never entirely mean what we say, do we? Do I mean that? Not entirely. And logically it follows that when we say we don't mean what we say, only then are we entirely serious.

VERONICA: Except we're not in England, darling.

DUFF: I see England now in grammatical terms almost as a tense, a mood. The optative. Would that this were so. Would it were different. But, of course, that will change. It will be different.

HILARY: I am so out of it. Fourteen years. I am a stranger.

DUFF: Precisely. So who better. You return from exile with a new perspective. So fruitful, exile. But then all writers are exiles here, are they not? Exiles in their own country. Which is where (dare one say it) our friend Solzhenitsyn made his mistake. I'm afraid they were in some sense right: he does want his head examining. Here he was. Grand. Isolated.

Attended to. A man as majestic and romantic as Byron. A torch. Drawing all eyes (all eyes that mattered. All *caring* eyes.) And he throws it away. Switzerland. Connecticut. He should have stayed put.

BRON: And gone to a camp?

DUFF: My dear Bron. Which is better, five years in a camp or three pages in *The Listener*? Fool. I thought (we had a reception for him at Chatham House) Fool. And a tendency already to button-hole. Sad. A talent betrayed.

HILARY: He was never someone one came across. What you are saying . . . let us spell it out . . . he has gone into exile and betrayed his talent. I am to return from exile and fulfil mine. Is that it?

DUFF: Absolutely.

HILARY: There is just one thing. I don't have any.

DUFF: What?

HILARY: Talent.

DUFF: You are too modest.

HILARY: Literary talent. None.

DUFF: You have a story to tell. You must tell it. My publishers have several very bright young people down from university. Tell it to one of them.

HILARY: Isn't that cheating?

DUFF: Cheating? To tell it to the tape recorder, and let the editor do the rest: my dear, what else is film. There are no categories. Form is in the melting pot. My publishers have brought out several vivid and successful books by an ex-housemaid. Has she talent? Content is what counts. Style can come later.

BRON: Don't take away his style or there'll be no content left.

HILARY: And where are they, your publishers?

DUFF: Bedford Square.

HILARY: Bedford Square. Is that handy for Portland Place? I suppose it is. No, I don't think so. Not really. Do you? Frankly Duff I don't think I'm cut out for literature. I don't know whatever made you think I was. The real artist confronts the world saying, 'Why am I not immortal?' 'Why am I second-rate?' is not the same question.

DUFF: My dear, dear man. You can be second rate and still be first class. Carve it above the door of the Slade. The Foreign Office. Oxford. The Treasury. Any institution you care to name. Draw the curtains. Pull up a chair. This is the family. Comfort. Charm. Humour. None of them negligible. What makes life worth living. None of that with jagged dirty genius on the hearthrug. No. The good is better than the best, else what does society mean?

BRON: Dear Duff.

HILARY: Dear Duff. You are so kind. (*Pause.*)

VERONICA: And when you bolted was it planned?

HILARY: Not a bit. All very much on spec. It was a Friday. I got back to the Foreign Office after lunch to find a note on my desk. It was in a brown, government envelope marked Urgent, underlined and with two exclamation marks. How dare the writer even of a brief note in dramatic circumstances be so confident of my amazement as to add an exclamation mark? And here were two of the buggers! It was a literary reference. *Great Expectations*, it read; then, in parentheses (and somewhat condescendingly), Dickens. Chapter 44. Wemmick's Warning. And another *bloody* exclamation mark. My first thought was, 'Who is this . . . person, this . . . well-wisher, this *friend*, who knows me so little as not to know how cross the medium of this message would make me. To say nothing of the punctuation.

DUFF: I thought you liked crosswords.

HILARY: I do. Provided they are set properly. The easier the crossword, the sloppier the clue. This was a sloppy clue.

VERONICA: Could you solve it?

HILARY: No. We were put to Dickens as children but it never quite took. That unremitting humanity soon had me cheesed off. I prefer Trollope. So on that Friday afternoon I scoured Whitehall for a copy of *Great Expectations* finally running one to earth in the lending library at the Army and Navy Stores. Is that still there?

DUFF: The Army and Navy? Oh yes.

HILARY: The Lending Library.

DUFF: No.

HILARY: Is there no end to your lunacy? The lending library at the Army and Navy! Senseless.

VERONICA: And what is Wemmick's warning?

DUFF: Do not go home. A note left for Pip at the gate of his lodgings and read by the light of the watchman's lantern.

HILARY: Do not go home.

VERONICA: That's straightforward enough.

HILARY: On the contrary. It's riddled with ambiguity. Home? Which home? I had three. Hookham, Newport Street or Cadogan Square. I always called Newport Street Newport Street, Cadogan Square Cadogan Square. The only place I had ever called home (because it was where Pa lived) was Hookham.

VERONICA: So where did you go?

HILARY: Hookham.

BRON: I was sitting in the garden. I was reading a thriller. I had just come to an intriguing part when Hilary arrived. Within ten minutes we had left.

VERONICA: And who was it tipped you off?

HILARY: It could have been anybody.

DUFF: Anybody brought up on Forster. 'If I had to choose between betraying my country and betraying my friend I hope I should have the guts to betray my country.'

VERONICA: The old boy must have had nice friends. I'd plump for the old Union Jack any day.

HILARY: All that's rubbish anyway.

DUFF: Hilary.

HILARY: Nancy rubbish. You only have to substitute 'my wife' for 'my friend' to find it's nothing like as noble. 'If I had to choose between betraying my country and betraying my wife I hope I should have the guts to betray my country.' Well . . . yes. I should hope so too. Wouldn't most people? And put the other way round it's sheer music hall. 'If I had to choose between betraying my country and betraying my wife I should betray my wife.' 'Your wife?' 'My wife.' 'Kindly leave the country.' If I had to choose between betraying my country and betraying my children I hope I should have the guts to betray my country. *Guts?* Or. If I

had to choose between betraying my country and betraying
. . . my brother-in-law . . . No, you see Duff. Friend is
what does it. My friend. That's what brings in the cellos.
My friend. Who is my friend? My friend is the memory of
the youth half of them were gone on at school. My friend is
True Love as it presents itself the one and only time in
their stunted, little lives in the shape of some fourteen-year-
old tart giving them the glad eye during the service of Nine
Lessons and Carols. And then of course they did have a
choice, if they had but known it. If only in the matter of a
kiss in the long grass behind the sightscreens. A choice
between country, which is to say school, headmaster,
government club and class; and fidelity, which is to say
friendship, honour, compassion and all the other virtues
which, if they were going to get anywhere at all in the world
they were going to have to betray anyway.

BRON: They? You. Us.

HILARY: No. That is their game and I have never played it.

BRON: But not wives. They never get a look in. Wives are part
of the betrayal. Wives are part of the selling-out. Wives are
settling for something. Do not go home. Do not settle
down. 'Leave for Cape Wrath tonight.'

VERONICA: And your friend, whoever he was?

HILARY: Unknown and unthanked.

DUFF: He certainly did you a good turn.

HILARY: Possibly. Possibly. After all we weren't entirely welcome
here either. Like the unlooked for arrival of a distant
relative from Australia. Naturally they made the best of it.
Kitted us out. Job. Flat. Not unpleasant. But a good turn
would you say, Bron? Not entirely.

VERONICA: So come back.

DUFF: Let me come clean. There have been several occasions this
last year (so different is the atmosphere nowadays) when one
or two of us have been sitting around, powers that be in a
mood of relaxation when quite independently your name has
come up. And people have suddenly started scratching their
heads and saying, 'What are we going to do about old
Hilary?' You've been stuck here now for what, thirteen,

fourteen years. Fourteen years *in partibus infidelium,* and
the upshot is, some of us are now prepared to come out and
say enough is enough. Now I can't quite say, 'Come home.
All is forgiven.' There are still one or two people who feel
quite strongly. Time dwindles their number but the fact
remains, there were deaths, disappearances. People . . .
died. Some of them first class. And I think you will
probably be made to stand in the corner for three or four
years, five at the outside, which with remission means three,
which with parole would probably be two and in one of
these open places (I'm on the board of a couple) more
hydros than houses of correction. Librarian pushing your
trolly round. Rather fun, I would have thought. Then once
that's out of the way you can get a little place somewhere.
Gloucestershire would be nice, handy for Bath. They've got
a delightful festival now . . . and Bristol, the Old Vic,
restaurants galore; England's changed since your day, all
sorts of places now where you can get a really first-class
meal. And financially, of course, no more problems.
Television, the Sundays, people falling over themselves. You
could even write this book you were talking about. Set up
your stall in the open market. I guarantee you'll have plenty
of customers. Granted some people are going to turn their
backs, but we live in a pluralist society and what does that
mean: it means somebody somewhere loves you. What do
you say?

BRON: You're wasting your time.

VERONICA: Did you know?

BRON: No.

HILARY: She never asked.

BRON: Because I never dreamed. What had it to do with me?
You think your husband is in central heating. You find out
he is in refrigerators. A commercial traveller toting his cheap
little case of samples round the suburbs. Little appoint-
ments. Rickmansworth. Ruislip. Dollis Hill.

HILARY: Not Dollis Hill. Never Dollis Hill. I give you Ruislip,
Pinner. But not Dollis Hill.

BRON: What does it matter?

HILARY: My wife has no sense of place. To her one spot is very much like another. It matters to me. It was my rendezvous. The top of my week. My epiphany. But hardly a double life. About as double as yours is double, Duff. The inner life of personal relations. The outer life of anagrams and Ongar. I say Ongar. Ruislip. Meetings at line's ending.

DUFF: At the station?

HILARY: Thereabouts. I used to walk from the station. Always walked. I took my umbrella, strode out into the suburbs and really revelled in it. Priestley, Duff. Wells. A little man on the loose. Past the ideal homes and Green Line bus stops. Factory sportsfields lined with poplars. I was so *happy*. Is it still unloved, that landscape? I loved it. Boarding kennels, down-at-heel riding schools, damp bungalows in wizened orchards. The metropolis tailing off into these forlorn enterprises. And not inappropriate. Had my superiors been blessed with irony I might have thought the setting deliberately chosen to point up the folly of individual endeavour. As it was I grew fond of it. And just as well. Shacks, allotments, dead ground. So many places like that now. Here. Africa. Soon, already, Arabia. Well, it suits me. At home in one you can be at home in them all.

DUFF: Forgive me, but am I fanciful if I begin to see your defection, say rather your odyssey in terms almost of a choice of *setting*? The heart of the country. The edge of the city. Two worlds. Past. Future. Not difficult to betray your country in so drab a setting for that setting has already betrayed the country you stood for: the house in the park, the church in the trees. No. Well. Possibly not.

HILARY: Is it a programme note that you want? Extracts from pertinent texts to point you in the right direction. Shots of the Depression, the upper classes at play. Injustice the impetus, the guilt of one's breeding. Neat. Good intentioned. The best motives gone wrong. Would that find favour?

DUFF: It's not unfamiliar. The road many took. Though few went so far.

VERONICA: I always knew you were a big Stalin fan.

HILARY: You seem anxious to nudge me into some sort of credo.

VERONICA: Well what about this mess on the carpet, which we've had to live with for fifteen years. When you've lowered your pinstripes and carefully done your No. 2's right in the middle of the hearth-rug one is entitled to some explanation. It would be nice to think this turd had an infrastructure.

HILARY: Talking of credos, do you know that in the latest recension of the creed one doesn't say 'I believe in God' but '*We* believe in God?' I've never heard such vulgar nonsense. The Archbishop of Canterbury should be shot.

We believe. How am I to know what anyone else believes? But does one have a choice between systems? This mode or that, an institutional best buy? When? At Cambridge? Or before that? The nursery perhaps. (My first taste of an institution that was on the decline.) I don't count the family. I believe that's now suffering from planning blight. Done out of devilment, would that meet with sympathy? To be on one's own. Alone. If for no other reason than to be one's own worst enemy.

VERONICA: You were always that.

BRON: Only just.

HILARY: It's quite hard to be absolutely alone. I never have. Though I have seen it. One particular afternoon I had been on one of my little jaunts, kept my appointment. Nothing unusual had occurred or was in the least likely to occur. It was a routine Thursday and I strolled back to the station across a piece of waste ground that I knew made a nice short cut. I must have seemed a slightly incongruous figure in my city clothes. I never dressed the part, even to the extent of an old raincoat. At which point I came over the brow of the hill and found myself facing a line of policemen, advancing slowly through the undergrowth, poking in ditches with long sticks, hunting for something. It appeared there was a child missing, believed dead. Clothes had been found; a shoe. It was a bad moment. I had no reason at all for being there. I was a senior official in the Foreign Office. What was I doing on a spring afternoon, with documents in my briefcase, crossing a common where a child had been murdered? As it was no one thought to ask me any questions at all. I looked too respectable. And indeed they already had a suspect waiting handcuffed in the police car. I joined in the search and was with them when they found the child about half an hour later, lying in a heap at the foot of a wall. I just got a glimpse of her legs, white, like mushrooms, before they threw a blanket over her. She had been dead a week. I saw the man as the police car drew away through lines of jeering housewives and people cycling home from work. Then they threw a blanket over him too. The handy blanket. And I have a feeling he was eventually hanged. Anyway it was in those days. I came back, replaced the documents, had my tea by the fire in the Foreign Office. I took in some parliamentary questions for the minister, had dinner at the Garrick and walked home across the park. And in a tiled room at Uxbridge Police Station there would have been that young man waiting. Alone in a cell. Alone in custody. Alone at large. A man without home or haven. That is what you have to do to be cast out. Murder children. Nothing else quite does the trick, because any other crime will always find you friends. Rape them, kill them and be caught.

(ERIC *enters.*)

Then there is no refuge, even in prison.

ERIC: There's a car at the end of the track. They looked at my papers. Has anything happened?

HILARY: What sort of car?

ERIC: Security men. Have they been here?

BRON: Here? Nobody's been here.

HILARY: Apart from our visitors. This is Eric, Duff. Eric, Veronica. Our young friend.

ERIC: I'm sorry to spring myself on you. Only Olga wanted to call in.

HILARY: Olga? Why? Perhaps we should stroll down.

BRON: No.

HILARY: Why not? Duff?

DUFF: I won't if you don't mind.

HILARY: It's always good for a laugh. V?

VERONICA: I'm game. I'm game for anything.

    (HILARY *and* VERONICA *go.*)

BRON: Where is Olga?

ERIC: Down there.

BRON: I'd better go too.

    (DUFF *looks at a book.*)

DUFF: Yes. Ye-es. (*Turning decisively into the room.*) Yes.

ERIC: Have you ever been here before?

DUFF: No. No, I haven't. I've never had a particular reason. I've never had the *yen*. I suppose if I were pressed for a reason I would have to say that I came to Slavonic art only comparatively recently. Yes. Art. That after all is what tempts us out of doors. Beckons us across the street. Across continents. Greece. Italy. Ceylon. Art is the magnet. That is why I have never been to Jersey. Or the Isle of Man. And very seldom to Wales. One can't see them from here?

ERIC: No.

DUFF: The museums here are stuffed with good things. The Impressionists are *staggering*. And most of them, one suspects, wasted.

ERIC: We've met before.

    (DUFF *smiles.*)

    At home.

DUFF: At home. And where is that? Home?

ERIC: Gosport. London.

DUFF: Gosport. No. I think it unlikely. You have seen my face in the press. I am on the Arts Council, a member of several working parties. Occasionally one creeps into the headlines.

ERIC: You took me back to your flat.

DUFF: Lately I have been active in promoting some new form of remuneration for the writers of fiction. The outlook for the novel has never been so bleak. I have no flat. I live in St John's Wood.

ERIC: You were very nice to me. I stayed the night.

DUFF: Novels. Poetry. One marvels they get written at all. You spent the night? I don't think so. I have a daughter at Warwick University.

ERIC: It was in the National Gallery one Sunday afternoon.

54

DUFF: Weekends invariably find me in Wiltshire.

ERIC: I don't understand all that. People trooping round. I never know which pictures to stop at. I end up looking at pictures I've seen pictures of because I think they must be the best.

DUFF: Why not? Why not? They probably are. Tried. Tested. I propounded a scheme not long ago (rejected solely on grounds of cost) for galleries to print little flags. Stickers. Of the sort . . . Skegness, Luxembourg . . . you see on Dormobile windows. Why not 'The Laughing Cavalier', 'The Hay Wain', 'We have see the Wallace Collection'. On the lines 'We have seen the lions of Longleat'. We must not be afraid to take art into the market-place.

ERIC: Have you seen those?

DUFF: What?

ERIC: The lions of Longleat?

DUFF: No. No.

ERIC: We have. My wife and I. I'm married, too.

DUFF: Too? You are certainly thinking of someone else.

ERIC: I had a bit of a moustache then. You were thinner.

DUFF: One was always thinner.

ERIC: It was you.

DUFF: What can be keeping him? One hopes our host hasn't done anything foolish. The art form hardest to justify in cost-benefit terms is of course opera. On the board of the Royal Opera we are very much aware of this. I never go into Covent Garden, which of course I do constantly, without some feeling if not of actual guilt at any rate certainly of it not being entirely fair. Feelings somewhat allayed now that we have introduced our promenade evenings with tickets to fit the pocket of the office worker. The shop assistant. The bank clerk. In a word Young People. To be young, that is the privilege. What is a box at the opera? What is a seat in the stalls? A cushion. Part of the upholstery of life. What it is not is youth. Beauty.

ERIC: I thought you just wanted a go in the bogs. Instead you took me back and gave me some tea and I spent the evening sat in my underpants looking at *Country Life*. It was really civilised.

DUFF: That is something I never do, if I want to sleep at night.
Look at the back numbers of *Country Life*. The properties.
Palaces practically. Sold, for nothing. Ten, even five years
ago. Had one but known. No. No. That way madness lies.
As for this other I am not sure what is being required.
Corroboration, is it? Or nostalgia. Hardly an idyll. And very
Angus Wilson.

ERIC: Who's he?

DUFF: Angus Wilson is a . . . never mind. Have you the correct
time? We have a car coming at five.

ERIC: It's just that I'd like to come home.

DUFF: I was warned against blackmail.

ERIC: Not blackmail. Old times.

DUFF: It is old times, all that. Cuts no ice nowadays.

ERIC: You could pull strings. You know people.

DUFF: What makes you think that? I am virtually a recluse.

ERIC: No.

DUFF: A lackey. A mere *fonctionnaire*. We are talking about the
Law. Authority. The immutables. Here you are, and here,
short of a radical alteration, you will have to stay.

ERIC: You're just a prick.

DUFF: I think I hear the party returning.

ERIC: It's not fair.

DUFF: It is a distasteful fact but I am fifty-six. You are in Russia.
Neither of us can go back. We must both make ourselves at
home.

ERIC: It's not the same.

DUFF: Why is it not the same?

ERIC: I don't know. Because . . . it's not my fault I'm here.

DUFF: Fault. Fault. It's not my fault I'm fifty-six. Time . . . just
went. It dribbled away.

ERIC: You had your life. What have I had?

DUFF: We must both of us strive after resignation. We all have
to be somewhere.

ERIC: Pisspot.

(*Enter* VERONICA.)

VERONICA: I see we've broken the ice.

DUFF: What precisely is happening?

VERONICA: Nothing. A black car. Four men in overcoats looking like commissionaires. 'Have you any jeans?' Nothing very ominous at all. They talked to your wife.

ERIC: They would.

DUFF: What did Hilary say?

VERONICA: Big joke. What time is our car coming?

DUFF: Soon. On schedule. Our friend would like to go with us.

VERONICA: To Moscow?

DUFF: Home.

VERONICA: Why is that?

DUFF: It appears he is not happy here. He is homesick. I've told him he must buckle to. One can't be flitting about the world just because one isn't happy. One would never be still.

VERONICA: Anyway you wouldn't recognise London. London's frightful. So smelly. Onions. Fried chicken, that sort of thing. Your wife on the other hand seems at home here. Chatting.

ERIC: She was at home in Holloway.

DUFF: Was it Holloway? I know the Governor there. Delightful woman. And a lion in committee. I must find out if they ran across each other.

ERIC: I was in Wakefield.

DUFF: Yes. That's quite a small gaol, isn't it. I don't actually know it. I know the bishop. Splendid man. One of these train fanatics.

(HILARY *enters with* BRON.)

HILARY: I should have been a bishop by now, if I'd taken orders.

DUFF: What of our friends? Were they forthcoming?

HILARY: One gathers it's a routine visitation. In that line of work there's very little that isn't routine.

VERONICA: Including pulling finger-nails out.

HILARY: I think you'd find that's rather old-fashioned. It's curious, isn't it, that whereas the man who gets pleasure out of his job will generally do it better, a torturer who gets pleasure out of it will invariably do it worse. It has to be routine. Though of course I don't believe it happens. Oh. Curiouser and curiouser. He's got a little friend.

57

BRON: Hilary. What is happening?

HILARY: We seem to be the object of some attention. Now why is that, Duffy? I hope you've been behaving yourselves.

DUFF: Our car is coming at five, and we're bidden to the ballet this evening so we have a fairly tight schedule. I must ask you again. As a friend. Will you come back? It isn't an idle question.

HILARY: Oh. I thought it was. 'Slot it in at the back of your mind,' you said. However. I have to decide. Come down on one side or the other. And without recourse to irony. Which is not to decide at all but have it both ways. The English speciality. I wonder with the new European vogue that we don't have a referendum on it. Irony, is it a good thing? And on the voting paper two boxes, one to read Yes or No. The other Yes *and* No. The whole thing would have to be held under the auspices of an institution impervious to irony . . . the Egg Marketing Board suggests itself, or the Royal School of Needlework. Except there is the problem: no institution you can name but the choice is tinged with irony. Utterly absent, it is never more present. Irony is inescapable. We're conceived in irony. We float in it from the womb. It's the amniotic fluid. It's the silver sea. It's the waters at their priestlike task washing away guilt and purpose and responsibility. Joking but not joking. Caring but not caring. Serious but not serious.

DUFF: I am serious. It is serious.

HILARY: Bron?

BRON: Why ask me?

HILARY: Weigh it all up. No Gamages. No Pontings. No more trains from Kemble to Cirencester. No Lyons. On the other hand I read of the renaissance of the small bakery; country breweries revive. Better bread, better beer. They come from Florence to shop in Marks and Spencer. It is not an easy decision.

BRON: You never get tired of it, do you? Shoving your arse out of the car window. Pissing on the Cenotaph. Spitting on the graves. People died. And not merely died. Eventually died. Good people. Friends.

58

HILARY: That is true. It isn't altogether fair, but it's true.

DUFF: (*Blandly*) Dear Bron. To talk of guilt in a world where the purchase of an orange, for instance, is fraught with implications . . . the endorsement of tyranny, the sweating of labour . . . to talk of guilt in a world where the individual is incapable of calculating the economic consequence of his simplest action . . . is to talk of the air we breathe. Yes. There are germs in the air. Microbes. But how should they be eliminated. And if they should be, would we find ourselves to have been dependent on those microbes for the condition of our lives? We would. So let there be no talk of guilt at this juncture. As soon talk of cause and effect.

(*During this speech* HILARY *has been looking for a book.*)

HILARY: Talking of microbes I was reading somewhere that there are more microbes *per person* than the entire population of the world. Imagine that. Per *person*. This means that if the time scale is diminished in proportion to that of space it would be quite possible for the whole story of Greece and Rome to be played out between farts.

DUFF: Hilary.

HILARY: How can I come home? I am home. I am a Soviet citizen.

VERONICA: I didn't know that.

HILARY: Duff did.

DUFF: A technicality. To do with ordinary people.

VERONICA: Since when?

DUFF: 1939. The Nazi-Soviet pact.

VERONICA: A curious time to choose.

BRON: What do you expect?

DUFF: You see we could go today. Now. When the car comes. I think you'll find that there won't be any problem with your people here. Rather the reverse.

HILARY: I see. Hence our friends in the garden. With Olga.

DUFF: It would be convenient. For everyone.

HILARY: Have I a choice?

DUFF: You would be doing me a great personal favour.

HILARY: But have I a choice?

DUFF: When has one a choice? I am your friend. If you felt you had it would be . . . nice.

(*Enter* OLGA *from the garden.*)

OLGA: (*To* DUFF) But they are not ready.

BRON: We haven't quite decided yet.

OLGA: You had better get ready. There will be two cars. You will go in the first car. The others in the second car.

DUFF: I wanted him to feel it was his decision. I should have felt easier if it had been your decision. You would have felt better.

OLGA: We don't have time for any of that.

DUFF: One didn't want a scene.

OLGA: The British have someone we want. We have no one they especially want. But you will do.

DUFF: You and a disgruntled flautist who is also coming out. Denied opportunity to practise. Works on the roads. Sounds a little second rate to me.

HILARY: It's funny that the word that best describes all these disaffected people is 'Bolshy'. I'll be of no use to you. I have no information other than what I read in the English newspapers. And if I had, who would believe me now?

DUFF: No. No. I'm sure. No. It's none of that. None of that at all. Just think of it as a gesture. A tidying up. Part of the spin-off of détente.

OLGA: Anyway you are sixty-five.

BRON: Sixty-four.

OLGA: The age of retirement.

VERONICA: It'll be nice to have you home.

HILARY: Home. The dustbin.

DUFF: That happens to us all. I did so much want it to be your decision.

ERIC: What about me?

DUFF: It makes everyone feel better. Me. You. People at home. Coming home to face the music, *sua voluntate* as it were. That will strike a chord. But willy nilly arrangements had to be made. Security are so tedious. You will be handed over on Tuesday at Vienna.

ERIC: What about me?

DUFF: I'm longing to see their new *Cosi* but I don't think that there'll be time. You don't care for opera, do you?

HILARY: No.

DUFF: Pity. It's another world.

BRON: Nobody really wanted us here from the start.

VERONICA: Well, you don't want to stay where you're not wanted.

HILARY: I do. That's the only place I feel at home. And what about you, liebchen. When will they send you home?

OLGA: I have no home. Here is home.

HILARY: For how long? Jewish bitch.

DUFF: On the contrary, this lady has been very helpful.

BRON: What about Eric?

DUFF: That's not for me to say. We have this lady's feelings to consider.

OLGA: You should pack. If the cars are on schedule you have five minutes.

VERONICA: Is there anything I can do?

BRON: No, I'm getting used to it. (*She goes off.*)

HILARY: Did I tell you the joke about why is a mushroom like working for the party?

(*Pause.*)

I did, didn't I?

VERONICA: Yes.

(HILARY *wanders round among the books.*)

HILARY: We've forgotten now . . . it's too recent to remember . . . that for a short period just after the war England seemed on the verge of a Christian revival. Eliot, Fry. The converted Auden. God was suddenly quite smart. The same people who'd felt vaguely benevolent towards communism in the 30's now felt as kindly, and as vaguely, towards its antithesis.

VERONICA: I hope you don't think I knew about this. Nobody tells mother.

ERIC: I wouldn't mind going back to prison. That wouldn't bother me.

DUFF: Do you know how much it costs to keep a man in prison? Something in the region of £150 a week. From a cost-benefit point of view prisons should be scrapped tomorrow and the prisoners put up in Trust Houses. Do them just as much good.

ERIC: You can talk. He's a puff!

BRON: Eric.

ERIC: Who's embarrassed now?

HILARY: If my hands were to be cut off and put in a bucket with a lot of other hands, and someone said, 'Now pick out yours,' I don't think I'd know them.

(*Pause.*)

BRON: I would.

HILARY: We shall be able to go to church. Although I gather they've got rid of the old Eucharist and are experimenting with something called Series 1, Series 2 and Series 3. That doesn't sound like religion to me.

(*Pause.*)

It sounds like baseball. Did you go to church, ever?

ERIC: A bit. But only for the ping-pong. The vicar used to lock up the bats. That's not Christianity, is it?

HILARY: Moscow comes under the diocese of Fulham. Ever come across him, Duff? Barry, our Bishop. One of these ecumenical merchants. All join hands. Forget our differences. No fear.

DUFF: No sign of them?

HILARY: A nice book would be the Anglican church in Europe. Riviera vicars. Embassy curates. A rich haul of eccentrics. Incidentally, does the embassy have a chaplain?

DUFF: No.

HILARY: How on earth do they manage?

VERONICA: What happened to the ban on irony?

HILARY: That's the dilemma. Its presence is intolerable, its absence inexcusable. Where you could set my mind at rest, Duff. Or you, Veronica is whether (having paid the penalty, wiped the slate clean, whatever) I will still be in time to catch a decent afternoon tea. By that I mean tea, bread and butter, scones and jam. Not to mention Fuller's walnut cake.

BRON: Oh stop it. Stop it. You've no need to keep it up now.

HILARY: Nothing to keep up, as you should know by now. The best disguise of all is to be exactly what you say you are.

Nobody ever believes that.

DUFF: No sign.

OLGA: No.

ERIC: If she really cared about me she'd want what I wanted.

BRON: Eric.

ERIC: Don't keep saying, 'Eric, Eric.' That doesn't mean anything either. You're no different from her. What am I going to do?

HILARY: Well, there's a pistol in that drawer.

BRON: I don't know. Maybe you ought to get a dog.

HILARY: I believe some people commit suicide out of sheer curiosity. Certainly if one were to cut one's throat I think the first thought as blood spurted through one's fingers would be, 'Goodness! It works!' Exclamation mark. Now Duff, what about my books?

DUFF: I foresee no difficulty. They will be home almost as soon as you are.

HILARY: That's what I'm worried about. I think I ought to leave them here.

DUFF: It would please the British Council. The Embassy is barren of books.

HILARY: I wasn't thinking of the Embassy. I was thinking of Eric.

DUFF: Eric?

HILARY: Someone must. You see it's all here, Eric. *Horizon*, the parish magazine. *Scrutiny*, the school chronicle. All the nice distinctions, careful cross-bearings and distances on the pedometer. Relief maps of anxiety, the contours of small depressions. Get well cards and invites to funerals. Notes under the general heading of amelioration. Deaths in vicarages and (Little) Venice. Bottles of Jordan water and basinfuls of the warm south. School and the trenches, good talk and good wine and the never-ending siege of the country house. Messages from an unvisited island. What would the Ambassador want with all that? He is a cultivated fellow. He can take it as read. But it's just what Eric wants.

ERIC: I don't read.

HILARY: It will be something to do.

OLGA: He doesn't want the books.

ERIC: Yes, I do.

BRON: Why? Crosswords, anagrams. Detective stories. English nonsense.

HILARY: Why do you think I don't want them? It's Toad Hall.

BRON: It's all very well never to do what is expected of you, but what do you do when the unexpected is what people have come to expect?

HILARY: Then you do the done thing.

VERONICA: Make one person happy. Pa.

DUFF: I imagine the telephone is cut off, is it?

OLGA: Yes.

DUFF: Pity.

HILARY: Here we are again. A country house. The telephone out of order. The road blocked. A group of disgruntled people waiting for . . . what? Deliverance, is it? Judgement?

BRON: Will there be photographers at the other end? Press?

DUFF: I can't give you an absolute assurance on that. I hope not. I don't know.

OLGA: The cars are here.

DUFF: Good, good. This time on Tuesday we shall be in Wiltshire.

(DUFF *shepherds* BRON *and* VERONICA *out.* OLGA *waits. A car horn sounds, two short notes.*)

ERIC: I don't want the books. I don't want the bloody books.

(HILARY *takes no notice. The car horn sounds again.*)

HILARY: Poop-poop. Poop-poop.

(*The chair is still rocking as* HILARY *leaves, followed by* OLGA. ERIC *watches them from the verandah, the books still in his arms.*)

CURTAIN